WONDERFUL WORLD OF
ANIMALS

As a 2008 Milken Educator, I take the challenge of reviewing educational materials seriously. As I examined the Disney Learning series, I was impressed by the vivid graphics, captivating content, and introductory humor provided by the various Disney characters. But I decided I should take the material to the true experts, my third grade students, and listen to what they had to say. In their words, "The series is interesting. The books are really fun and eye-catching! They make me want to learn more. I can't wait until the books are in the bookstore!" They looked forward to receiving a new book from the series with as much anticipation as a birthday present or a holiday gift. Based on their expert opinion, this series will be a part of my classroom library. I may even purchase two sets to meet their demand.

Barbara Black
2008 Milken Educator
National Board Certified Teacher—Middle Childhood Generalist
Certified 2001/Renewed 2010

For information address Disney Press,
114 Fifth Avenue, New York, New York 10011-5690.

Visit www.disneybooks.com
Printed in China
ISBN 978-1-4231-4940-8
T425-2382-5-12153
First Edition
Written by Thea Feldman
Fact-checked by Barbara Berliner
All rights reserved.

CONTENTS

WELCOME TO THE

WONDERFUL WORLD OF
ANIMALS

ANIMALS ARE EVERYWHERE!

There are animals on land, in the sky, and in most of the world's bodies of water. Animals walk, crawl, run, fly, and swim somewhere on the planet, day and night.

MAMMALS

There are more than 5,000 species of mammal, including humans. A mammal is a warm-blooded animal covered with hair or fur. A warm-blooded animal has a body temperature that stays constant. The animal does not depend upon the sun to keep it warm. Mammal mothers nurse their babies by feeding them milk. They take care of them until the young are able to live independently. Most mammals live on land, but there are some that spend most or all of their time in water. There is even one family of mammals that flies!

BIRDS

Just because you're a bird doesn't mean you can fly. You just need to be warm-blooded with feathers and wings. There are 9,900 bird species. Some take to the air part of the time. Several kinds of birds live on land. Others use their wings like flippers to swim the seas!

REPTILES

There are more than to 9,000 species of reptile on the planet. Reptiles are cold-blooded. They need the sun to heat their bodies and give them energy. A reptile's body is covered with scaly skin. Reptiles include snakes, lizards, turtles, and tortoises.

AMPHIBIANS

Amphibians are cold-blooded, too. An amphibian spends some of its time in water and some on land. Most adult amphibians actually breathe through their skin! To be able to do that, an amphibian has to keep its skin moist. That's why they can feel slimy when you touch them. Frogs, toads, and salamanders are some of the more than 6,400 species.

FISH

More than 30,000 species of fish swim in Earth's freshwater and saltwater bodies. A fish is a cold-blooded animal that breathes through gills. It moves through the water using fins.

ARCTIC

NORTH AMERICA

ATLANTIC

PACIFIC

SOUTH AMERICA

ANIMALS ON LAND

Earth is made up of seven continents and a few thousand islands. Most of these places support animal life. You'll find animals everywhere—from the coldest place on Earth (Antarctica) to the hottest desert.

EUROPE

ASIA

PACIFIC

AFRICA

INDIAN

AUSTRALIA

ANTARCTICA

WILD CATS

I'm in the mood for wildebeest today.

There are 37 species of wild cat in the world today. Wild cats have walked the Earth since prehistoric times.

Wild cats are carnivores (meat-eaters) with a hunter's instinct.

Lion

Siberian tiger

WHO IS THE **BIGGEST?**
WHO IS THE SMALLEST?

The **Siberian** or **amur tiger** is the largest species of wild cat. This cold-weather cat can weigh more than **800** pounds and grow to be 9 feet long! They are highly **endangered.** There are said to be less than 500 **Siberian** tigers left in the wild.

Don't be fooled by the **kittenish** look of the 3-to-4-pound, 25-inch-long **black-footed cat.** This little **predator** from the deserts of southern Africa is a skilled hunter of rodents, spiders, and insects. This cat gets its name from the black hairs on the bottom of its feet.

WHY ARE CATS SUCH **GOOD HUNTERS?**

Good hunters need great senses. Cats have large eyes, so they see over a wide area. A cat's **sense of smell** is about 30 times better than a human's and helps it locate food. Cats also have **excellent hearing.** The **African serval** is one wild cat that uses its keen sense of hearing to hunt.

Serval kitten

WHERE DO **WILD CATS LIVE?**

Wild cats are found in parts of Africa, Asia, the Middle East, Europe, and North, Central, and South America. They live in all kinds of **climates.** Some, such as the **jaguar,** are at home in lush, tropical jungles. Others, such as the **snow leopard,** live in **frigid** temperatures on rugged mountains.

Snow leopard

WILD DOGS

There are 36 species of wild dog. Most have large, upright ears, long, bushy tails, long snouts, and long legs.

We like meat!

All 36 species of wild dog are carnivores. Their jaws are strong and their teeth are sharp for killing and eating prey.

Fennecs

WHERE DO **WILD DOGS LIVE?**

Wild dogs are the most widespread of all **carnivores.** They are found all over the world, except in New Zealand and Antarctica, and on some islands. Wild dogs live in a variety of **habitats,** including forests and mountains. One species of fox, the **fennec,** makes its home in the hot deserts of the Sahara and the surrounding areas. The fennec burrows into the sand and sleeps during the day, when the temperature is at its hottest. In contrast, the **arctic fox** thrives in the cold northern tundra. Its thick coat and bushy tail help it stay warm.

Young spotted hyena

IN WHAT WAYS DO WILD DOGS **LIVE TOGETHER?**

Foxes tend to live in pairs or small family groups. Other species of **wild dogs,** including wolves, **hyenas,** coyotes, African wild dogs, and jackals, live in groups called **packs.** A pack can have more than 30 members. Every pack has a lead or **"alpha"** male and female in charge of the group. Every member of the pack has a job to do. Some raise the young and babysit to keep them **safe;** others go off and **hunt** together. A pack of wild dogs on the hunt can take down animals big enough for the whole pack to eat.

Gray wolf pack

BEARS

If you look at all eight species of bear, you'll see they look a lot alike. Bears rely more on their excellent sense of smell than on their hearing or vision.

Large head? Long nose? I'd say I *bear* a resemblance to bears!

Bears have very large heads with small, rounded ears, small eyes, and long noses. Their bodies are covered in long fur, including their very short tails.

Adult polar bear and cub

WHO IS THE BIGGEST BEAR? WHO IS THE SMALLEST?

The **polar bear** is the world's largest bear. A fully grown polar bear can weigh as much as **1,760 pounds** and grow to be over 8 feet tall (when standing on its hind legs). The **sun bear** is the smallest. A fully-grown sun bear weighs about **143 pounds** and is only about 4 feet, 9 inches tall.

Sun bear

Spirit bear

ARE ALL WHITE BEARS POLAR BEARS?

In British Columbia, **Canada,** there is a small population of bears with white fur that are not polar bears. Called **"spirit bears"** by locals, they are actually a rare kind of black bear! According to **legend,** these bears showed up when the world changed from being covered in white **glaciers** to being covered in green trees and plants. The legend says that **the Creator** made every tenth black bear white as a reminder of this earlier time. It's against the law to hunt these extra-special bears.

WHAT DO BEARS EAT?

Most bears are **omnivores.** They eat meat, plants, fruit, and berries. The exception is the **panda,** which eats mostly **bamboo.** In order to hold huge stalks of bamboo, the panda has an **extra digit** on each of its front paws to help it grip its food. A panda will eat about **45 pounds** of bamboo each day. That's the equivalent of 90 apples!

Giant panda

SNAKES, LIZARDS, AND FROGS

These reptiles and amphibians are deadly to both their prey and predators. They are also poisonous and can hurt or even kill a human!

I'm not afraid of any snakes!

Snakes live on every continent except Antarctica. And each continent has its share of deadly snakes.

Emerald tree boa

HOW DO SNAKES GET **THEIR PREY?**

Many snakes eat live prey. They simply snatch their meal and **swallow** it whole! Some snakes prefer to **squeeze** their prey to death first. These kinds of snakes are called **constrictors,** and they are the biggest snakes in the world. The longest constrictor—the **reticulated python**—can grow to be more than 29 feet long! Pythons usually eat monkeys, wild pigs, and deer, but they have been known to eat people on occasion.

Still other snakes stun or kill their prey with their **venomous fangs.** Just one bite from a **king cobra** is enough to kill an elephant!

Black mamba

WHERE DO SOME OF THE **DEADLIEST VENOMOUS** SNAKES LIVE?

Snakes live on every continent except **Antarctica. The black mamba** of Africa can move at a speedy 10 miles per hour, hunting rodents and small mammals. In Asia, the **Russell's viper** kills thousands of people each year. In Australia, the **inland taipan's** venom can kill a person in under an hour. The **eastern diamondback rattlesnake** is the largest venomous snake in North America.

Blue poison dart frog

WHAT FROGS ARE **DEADLY?**

They may look like tiny, living jewels, but the almost 200 species of **poison dart frog** have toxic skin. A person would die after eating one. These frogs are tiny—less than 2 inches long. They live in the tropical forests of Central and South America. The frogs are **brightly colored** to warn predators not to eat them. If that doesn't work, the **toxins** will make the predator spit the frog out!

King cobra

THAT'S REALLY WILD!

> Now there's a guy who will always stick his neck out for you!

SMALLEST ANIMAL ON LAND

Some crawling insects are so small we can't see them. These include feather-winged beetles and fungus beetles. A single **fungus beetle** is less than $\frac{1}{7}$ of an inch long. Thief ants can be even smaller—but they're still twice the size of some **dust mites,** which are about $\frac{1}{64}$ of an inch!

TALLEST ANIMAL ON LAND

A **giraffe** stands about 10 feet tall at the shoulder, which is about 2 feet shorter at the shoulder than an **African elephant.** But a giraffe's neck can add another 8 feet of height to its body! That makes the 18-foot-tall animal easily the world's tallest. A newborn giraffe already stands about 6 feet tall!

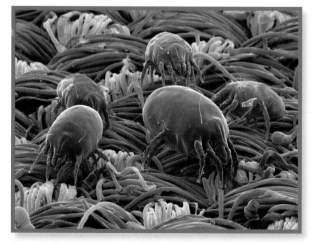

Dust mites, magnification x 300

FASCINATING LAND ANIMALS
AND SOME WORLD-RECORD HOLDERS, TOO!

HEAVIEST
ANIMAL ON LAND

The male **African elephant** is the world's **heaviest** land animal. An adult male can weigh more than **13,000 pounds.** That's heavier than 80 humans! This mammal also stands about 12 feet tall at the shoulder. A baby elephant weighs about **250 pounds** at birth—more than 35 times as much as most human babies!

African elephant

Radiated tortoise

LONGEST–LIVED
ANIMAL ON LAND

British explorer Captain James Cook presented a **Madagascar radiated tortoise** to the royal family of Tonga in 1777. Named King Malila, the animal lived with successive generations of the royal family until he died at the age of **188.** That makes him one of the **longest-lived** animals.

CRAWLING INSECTS

Scientists estimate there are about 900,000 different kinds of insect! What do they have in common? Every insect has three body parts and six legs.

Insects help keep plant growth in check, help keep the planet clean, and are food for other animals.

Monarch caterpillars

WHY DO INSECTS COME IN MY HOUSE?

Insects invade homes mostly to eat. **Silverfish,** wingless insects that grow to be no longer than three-quarters of an inch long, love to eat anything made from plants. They're happy with a meal of **glue** (including the kind used in book bindings), wallpaper paste, papers, photographs, and cotton or linen things, such as clothing and bed sheets. **Silverfish** may be **destructive** to your things and creepy to look at. But they won't hurt you.

In some parts of the world, **termites** chew on the wood inside the walls of houses. Their **munching** can cause a lot of damage to a house. And in the process of digesting wood, termites make and release methane gas!

Silverfish

Large termite mound

HOW DO INSECTS LIVE TOGETHER?

Many insect species are considered **"social"** animals. Several thousand of them may live together in a group (often called a **colony**). In Africa and Australia, thousands of **termites** live together in a home they build for themselves out of clay or soil. A termite mound can be as tall as a **three-story building!**

WHERE DO COCKROACHES LIVE?

There are more than **4,000 species** of **cockroach** crawling all over the planet. They live everywhere, even the Arctic. Only about two dozen species of cockroach ever come into contact with people. Those are generally considered to be **pests.** They seek out moist, dark, and damp places—kitchens, bathrooms, or basements. Cockroaches will eat almost anything, **even each other!**

WHY DO SOME INSECTS LIVE IN FURNITURE?

Some insects, such as **bedbugs,** hide in cracks in furniture or in the walls or floor. Bedbugs don't need to be near water or food because they prefer **human blood!** A baby bedbug will be about the size of a **poppy seed** when it first hatches. It will grow as big as an apple seed. When it bites a person's skin, a bedbug will **swell.** It will turn redder from the blood it dines on!

SPIDERS AND SCORPIONS

Spiders and scorpions are arachnids. An arachnid, like an insect, has an exoskeleton, which is a hard covering on the outside of its body.

Exoskeleton? Oh, shiny!

An arachnid has two body parts, eight legs, and no wings. There are nearly 50,000 species of spider and close to 1,500 species of scorpion.

Jumping spider with victim

Scorpion

WHERE DO **SPIDERS** AND **SCORPIONS LIVE?**

Spiders live everywhere on Earth except Antarctica; **scorpions** live everywhere except Antarctica and Greenland. Scorpions were once found mainly in deserts, but now they also live in tropical rain forests, other types of forests, and grasslands.

WHAT EXACTLY IS A **SPIDERWEB?**

A spiderweb is a **trap** for the spider's prey. A spider builds a web with **silk** it produces inside its own body! The silk comes out like thread through a tubelike opening in the spider's body called a **spinneret.** The silk threads are **sticky.** When an insect gets caught in a web, it will never get out!

Tandem spider catching fly in web

WHAT IS THE **BIGGEST** SPIDER?

The world's **biggest** spider is the **Goliath tarantula.** It can be almost as big as a **dinner plate!** Its legs alone can span 11 inches! The Goliath is found throughout the tropical rain forests of South America. They're not deadly to humans, but a bite from its one-inch-long fangs can be really **painful** and make you sick. A tarantula also has hairs all over its body that it will release if it feels threatened. These hairs can irritate a person's skin.

Goliath tarantula

WELL-ARMORED ANIMALS

Armadillos, porcupines, hedgehogs, echidnas, land tortoises, and land turtles are not related. But they do share the ability to protect themselves with their well-armored exteriors.

Respect a porcupine— from a distance!

Armadillo is Spanish for "little armored one." The name comes from the bony plates that cover its back.

Armadillo

WHY DO **HEDGEHOGS** AND **PORCUPINES** HAVE **SPINES?**

Hedgehogs and porcupines are covered in sharp **spines** or **quills** made out of **keratin.** Your hair and nails are made of the same thing! A scared hedgehog can make its sharp spines stand up. It can also roll itself into a **tight ball,** leaving nothing for a predator to bite but thousands of spines. A hedgehog will often sleep in this safe position as well.

Brazilian porcupine

Galapagos giant tortoise

WHAT MAMMALS LAY **EGGS?**

Echidnas and **duck-billed platypuses** are the only mammals that lay eggs instead of giving birth to live young. They are called **monotremes,** and they lay soft-shelled eggs that hatch after only 10 days. They take care of their young like other mammal mothers.

HOW DOES ITS SHELL KEEP A **LAND TORTOISE** OR A **TURTLE SAFE?**

A **tortoise** or turtle shell is made up of tough bony plates or scales called **scutes.** Most land tortoises have high, rounded shells that are hard for predators to bite or crush.

Turtles can pull their heads and legs into their shells for safety. A **box turtle** can also pull up its bottom shell to seal itself completely inside. **Predators** soon give up trying to bite their way in.

Echidna

SPRAYERS, SPITTERS, AND ANIMALS THAT OOZE

I've marked it all as mine!

Whether scared, mad, trying to stay alive, or sending a message, lots of animals let liquids do the talking!

A camel will spit out saliva and the entire contents of its stomach, as a surprise or distraction to a threat.

Dubai camel

Spittlebug larva

WHO IS A "SPITTER"?

There are more than 150 species of spitting spider around the world. These **spiders** build the usual webs to snare prey. But they can also **spit** a gluey substance at an approaching meal. The spit holds the prey in place, and the spider digs in.

The **spittlebug's** name says it all. It spits out thick, slightly sticky bubbles onto a leaf. The **spit bubbles** form a sturdy, protective home for the bug's young.

WHAT UNUSUAL FLUIDS DO ANIMALS SPRAY?

At least four of the 14 species of North American **horned lizard** share a unique way of getting rid of predators. They spray **blood** from their eyes! Blood can come out in a 5-foot-long stream. No surprise, predators find this disgusting.

Texas horned lizard

Baby skunk

WHAT ANIMALS SPRAY FOR SELF-DEFENSE?

The **skunk** is the first animal you think of when it comes to animals that spray. But a skunk will only **spray** when it feels threatened. Every skunk has two glands located beneath its tail. These contain a **foul-smelling liquid.** The spray not only smells bad, it burns, too!

25

ANIMALS
OF THE AIR

Air is all around us. It's above the land and over the water. Air is made up of a mixture of invisible gases, including oxygen, which all animals need to survive. Air has weight because of all those gases.

ARCTIC

NORTH AMERICA

ATLANTIC

PACIFIC

SOUTH AMERICA

BATS

Ha-ha! I'm a flying mammal, too!

There are more than 925 species of bat in the world, flying everywhere except for the Arctic and Antarctica.

Bats are the only flying mammals in the world, and they make up about 20% of all mammal species on Earth.

Mexican free-tailed bats

WHY DO BATS HANG **UPSIDE DOWN?**

Scientists think there are two reasons. The first has to do with the way a bat's body is built. A bat can't take off and fly the way a bird does by using its legs to help it get airborne. **It just lets go,** spreads its wings, and flies.

The second reason bats hang upside down may have to do with **keeping safe.** Predators usually can't reach **cave ceilings.**

Pallid bat

WHEN ARE BATS **ACTIVE?**

Bats are **nocturnal** animals. That means they are active at night.

Vampire bat

DO **BLOOD-SUCKING** BATS REALLY EXIST?

Vampire bats—blood-sucking bats—really do exist. There are three species of vampire bat. These live mainly in **Central** and **South America.** They don't suck human blood. They prefer blood from pigs, cows, horses, or poultry. The **common vampire bat** needs to eat about half its body weight in blood every night! The largest species, the **white-winged vampire bat,** weighs only about 1.5 ounces.

FLIES AND MOSQUITOES

Don't worry, he's as harmless as a fly!

Unlike other flying insects (which each have four wings), flies and mosquitoes only have two wings.

The 120,000 species of these insects don't have any trouble getting around. They seem to be everywhere—because they are!

Fruit fly

WHAT ELSE DO **FLIES** AND **MOSQUITOES** HAVE IN COMMON?

Flies and **mosquitoes** bring lots of **diseases** with them. Flies might land on your lunch after they have poked around in **decaying** animal feces, garbage, rotting food, or other **unsanitary** things.

There are 3,000 species of mosquito. Female **anopheles mosquitoes** are the deadliest creatures on Earth! They carry **malaria,** a disease that kills over two million people a year.

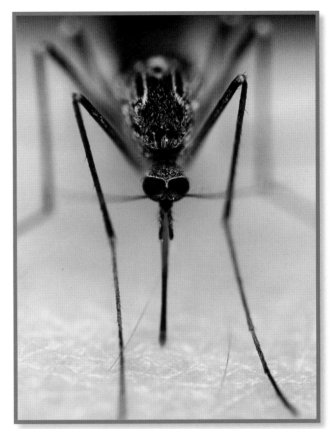
Mosquito

Tsetse fly

HOW DOES A FLY **EAT?**

Before a fly can eat, it **vomits** on its food! Flies can only eat food in liquid form. There are **chemicals** in their bodies that help turn solid things into **liquids.** So when a fly throws up, its food breaks down into a form the insect can lap up.

WHERE DOES A FLY **LAY ITS EGGS?**

Flies lay their eggs in garbage, fresh **manure,** or on the bodies of dead animals! The eggs hatch within a few hours. Soon, young flies, called **maggots,** begin to eat whatever it is they've hatched on. Maggots look more like **worms** than flies. They are legless and wingless. But, like adult flies, maggots can't eat solids. They release a **fluid** that turns their meal into a liquid.

Maggots

OWLS

The more than 200 species of owl are found on every continent except Antarctica. Most of the world's owls are nocturnal, meaning they sleep during the day and hunt at night.

Owls, like all other birds, have ear openings hidden underneath their feathers. Scientists think the tufts help owls communicate with one another, or help them blend into their surroundings.

Boreal owl

HOW DO OWLS **HUNT FOR FOOD?**

Owls hunt for **live prey.** They rely most on their excellent **vision** and **hearing** to find meals. Owls have special flight feathers that muffle sound, so their prey does not hear them coming. An owl will **swoop down** from the sky and grab rodents, other small mammals, fish, and even other birds in its **talons,** or claws. After using its talons or its sharp, curved beak to kill its prey, an owl will then swallow the meal whole.

HOW DO OWLS **EAT?**

An owl will **swallow** its prey whole, but it cannot digest the entire thing. An owl can't digest fur, feathers, and bones. So, it **compresses** these remains into tight **pellets** and regularly **vomits** them up. Scientists study owl pellets to determine what a particular species or bird has been eating.

Short-eared owls

Great horned owl

WHAT IS SPECIAL ABOUT AN OWL'S EYES?

One of the first things you notice when you look at an owl are its **enormous eyes** looking back at you! An owl's eyes allow it to see about **three times** better than a person. But it can't move its eyes around the way a person can. In order to see what's beside it, an owl has to **turn its head.** It can turn its entire head about three-quarters of the way around!

Snowy owl

EAGLES

Eagles are birds of prey. Also called raptors, birds of prey are the largest flying meat-eaters in the world.

A bird of prey hunts for live animals or fish. The bird uses its talons to capture and fly off with it. The bird of prey then squeezes its catch to death before ripping into the flesh with its sharp, curved beak.

Bald eagle in flight

WHERE DO EAGLES LIVE?

Eagles live on every continent except Antarctica. They can live in forests, deserts, mountain ranges, or **savannas.** Some, such as the **bald eagle,** live in the very cold Arctic region.

Golden eagle

Philippine eagle

HOW MANY KINDS OF EAGLES ARE THERE?

There are about 60 kinds of eagles, which belong to four different groups. **Booted eagles** have legs covered in feathers. The golden eagle of Europe and North America is a booted eagle. **Sea eagles,** including the bald eagle and Steller's sea eagle, usually live near bodies of water and eat fish. **Forest eagles,** including the Philippine eagle, mainly live in tropical rain forests. And snake or **serpent eagles** eat mostly reptiles. The black-chested snake eagle lives in Africa, where it eats snakes, lizards, frogs, and small mammals.

WHO ARE THE LARGEST EAGLES?

The **harpy eagle** lives in tropical forests in Central and South America. It is the world's largest eagle. It can grow to be over **3.5 feet** long and weigh nearly **20 pounds.** It eats animals that live in trees, such as sloths and monkeys. The wedge-tailed eagle of Australia can be over 3 feet long and weigh up to **12 pounds.** Its prey includes rabbits, young kangaroos, and **wallabies.** The **white-tailed eagle,** a sea eagle, is the largest in northern Europe. It can be almost 3 feet long and weigh up to 12 pounds. It **snatches** its catch from the surface of the water.

Wedge-tailed eaglets (baby eagles)

THAT'S REALLY WILL!

Bird and butterfly watching is fun!

FASTEST
FLYING INSECT

The **dragonfly** holds the record for speed, flying at **35** miles per hour. However, a dragonfly can't walk due to the position of its legs!

Pygmy blue butterfly

SMALLEST BUTTERFLY AND MOTH

The **pygmy blue** butterflies of the United States and the **dwarf blue** butterflies of South Africa are the world's smallest butterflies. Each has a **wingspan** of less than an inch. The world's smallest moths, **leaf-miner moths,** are even smaller, with a wingspan of less than $\frac{1}{10}$ of an inch. They are found worldwide.

LONGEST
BIRD BILL

The **Australian pelican's bill** can be **18.5** inches long. That's pretty long for a bird that is less than 6 feet long. An Australian pelican thrusts its bill **underwater** to grab fish, or it **scoops** up fish in shallow water.

FASCINATING ANIMALS THAT FLY
AND SOME WORLD-RECORD HOLDERS, TOO!

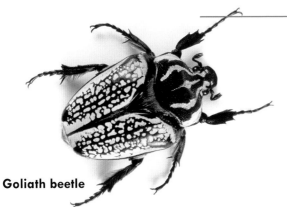

Goliath beetle

LARGEST
FLYING INSECT

The **Goliath beetle,** one of the world's largest beetles, is also the world's largest **flying** insect. It can reach 6 inches long and weigh 3.5 ounces.

LARGEST
BUTTERFLY AND MOTH

There are over **160,000** species of butterfly and moth in the world. How can you tell which one you're looking at? Butterflies are active during the day, and moths are active at night. The largest butterfly, the **Queen Alexandra's birdwing,** of the rain forests in Papua, New Guinea, is also one of the rarest. It has a wingspan of **12 inches. The atlas moth** is just as big. It is found throughout the jungles of Southeast Asia.

Atlas moth

POISONOUS BIRDS

The **hooded pitohui,** two other pitohui species, and the **blue-capped ifrita** are the world's only known **poisonous** birds. They have potent toxins in their skin and feathers. All live in the rain forests of New Guinea.

Hooded pitohui

VULTURES

The 22 species of vulture don't hunt live prey. They feast upon carrion, which is the flesh of a dead animal.

Carrion for breakfast? I like eggs instead!

Many vultures use their keen sense of smell to locate carrion. Other vultures find food using their sharp eyesight.

Turkey vulture

WHY DO SOME VULTURES HAVE **BALD HEADS?**

Vultures that don't have **feathers** on their heads tend to be the ones that stick their heads inside **carcasses.** If their heads had feathers, bits of decaying meat would get stuck in them.

The **king vulture** of Central and South America is not only bald, it has black, bright red, and yellow markings on its head and neck.

Lappet-faced vulture eating a wildebeest

HOW DO VULTURES WORK TO **GET A MEAL?**

The **griffon vulture** uses its long neck and beak to reach into a carcass and pull out the soft meat. The **bearded vulture** prefers to eat the marrow inside bones. It takes large bones in its beak, flies high, and drops the bones on rocks to break them and reach the soft marrow! Other vultures, such as the **lappet-faced vulture,** have beaks designed to break open a fresh carcass.

King vulture

HOW ELSE ARE VULTURES **DIFFERENT** FROM OTHER BIRDS OF PREY?

Because **vultures** don't catch live food, they don't need the strong legs and **sharp talons** other birds of prey have. They don't have to fly with their food. Instead, they fly *to* their food, using their long, strong almost **rectangular** wings.

Griffon vulture

OTHER BIRDS OF PREY

Over two dozen falcon species, including kestrels, are also birds of prey. So are hawks, kites, caracaras, buzzards, and ospreys.

Talk about a bird's-eye view!

Most birds of prey look for food from the sky and dive quickly toward it.
Peregrine falcon with prey

WHO ARE THE SMALLEST FALCONS?

The **Seychelles kestrel** is the world's smallest falcon. It can be 9 inches long and weigh slightly more than 3 ounces. This little bird lives in forests, including some **rain forests** on the Seychelles Islands. The second-smallest falcon is the **American kestrel.**

Kestrel

Crested caracara

HOW ELSE DO BIRDS OF PREY HUNT?

The northern **crested caracara,** found in the Americas, searches for food on the ground. It eats live reptiles and amphibians, as well as **carrion.** When this bird gets excited, the bare skin on its face **changes color!** It can turn from orange or red to bright yellow.

WHO ARE THE FASTEST BIRDS OF PREY?

The **peregrine falcon** is the world's **fastest** bird of prey. In the pursuit of its catch, a diving peregrine falcon can go up to **200** miles an hour! A peregrine falcon is a relatively small bird, about 20 inches long and weighing slightly more than 2 pounds. These birds mostly eat other birds, including **ducks, pigeons,** and **parrots.**

Peregrine falcon

NORTH
AMERICA

ATLANTIC

SOUTH
AMERICA

ANIMALS
IN WATER

More than 70% of our planet is covered in
water. Only 2.5% of that is freshwater—lakes,
rivers, streams, and ponds. The majority of
Earth's water is saltwater—the five oceans
that surround all landmasses. Fish live in
water, but many invertebrates, mammals,
birds, reptiles, and amphibians also call
water home.

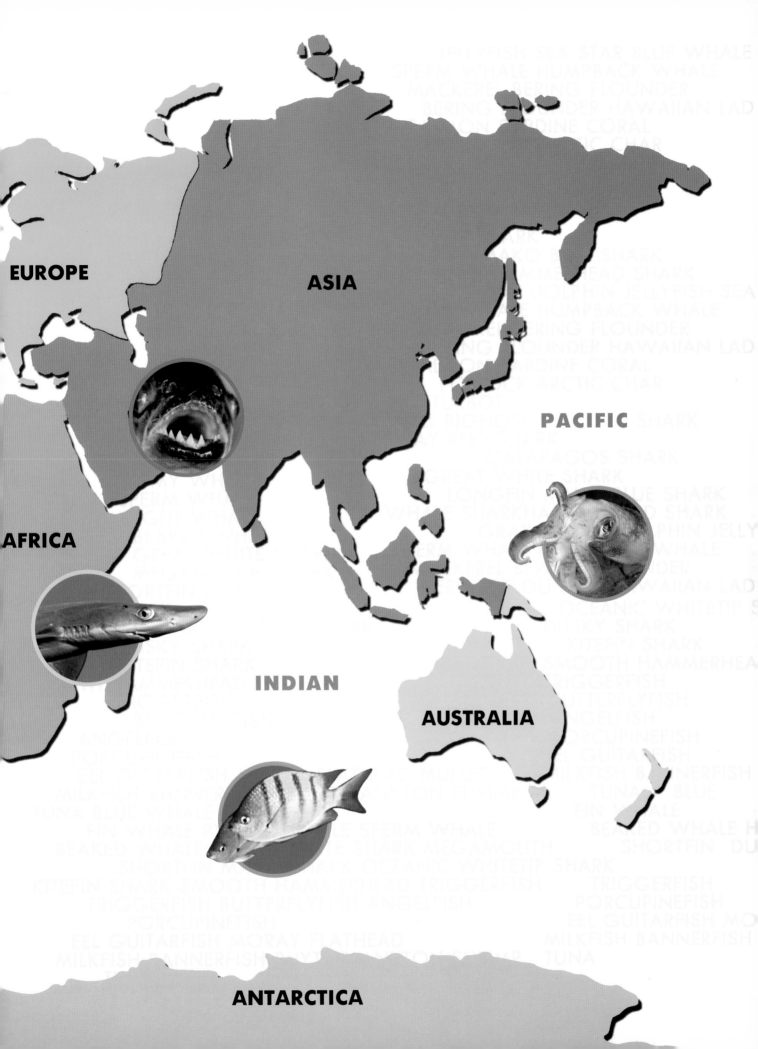

EUROPE

ASIA

PACIFIC

AFRICA

INDIAN

AUSTRALIA

ANTARCTICA

CROCODILIANS

Crocodilians are the world's largest reptiles. The 23 species of crocodile, gavial, alligator, and caiman have bodies covered with scales and big, powerful jaws containing short, crooked teeth.

Just keep swimming!

All crocodilians come out of the water to lay their eggs on land. The ancestors of crocodilians date back to the time of the dinosaurs.

Alligators

HOW MANY TEETH
ARE IN A CROCODILIAN'S MOUTH?

Crocodilians have at least twice as many **teeth** as adult humans do. People have 32 teeth. The **Nile crocodile** has 68 teeth. The **American alligator** has 80, and the **gavial** has over 100! And crocodilians can grow new teeth to replace any they lose.

Saltwater crocodile

American alligator

HOW DO CROCODILIANS HUNT?

Most **crocodilians** are **ambush predators.** They lie still in the water with eyes and noses above the surface, watching and waiting for prey to come near. They move quickly through the water, **propelled** by their tails, to grab a meal. Crocodilians eat all kinds of animals—fish, insects, birds, and even large mammals like zebras and **wildebeests.**

Some larger crocodiles are even capable of eating people!

WHO IS THE LARGEST CROCODILIAN?
WHO IS THE SMALLEST?

The **saltwater crocodile,** which patrols the waters between India and Australia, is the world's **largest** crocodilian. It's also the world's largest reptile. Adult males can be more than 20 feet long and weigh in excess of **2,200 pounds!** The saltwater crocodile will eat everything from insects to buffalo.

Cuvier's dwarf caiman of South America is the world's smallest crocodilian, reaching a maximum length of **5.2 feet.**

Dwarf caiman

SHARKS

Today there are about 400 species of shark swimming in the waters around the world.

I'm a nice shark, not a mindless eating machine!

The ancestors of sharks first appeared about 450 million years ago—that's about 200 million years before the dinosaurs!

Great white shark

WHO IS THE **LARGEST** SHARK? WHO IS THE SMALLEST?

The **whale shark** is the biggest. It can be **40 feet** long. Not bad for a creature that only eats plankton! Whale sharks swim in all warm and tropical seas except for the Mediterranean. The **great white** is the **largest predator** fish, though. The **smallest** shark is the **dwarf lantern** shark of the Caribbean. It only grows to be about as big as a dollar bill!

Whale shark

WHAT KIND OF ANIMALS ARE SHARKS?

Sharks are fish, but they have some unique features, including their **skeletal structures.** Most fish have hard skeletons, like people. Shark skeletons are made from a tough but flexible material called **cartilage.** Cartilage is lighter than bone and helps a shark get around quickly. The **short-fin mako shark** is the fastest shark. It can pursue its prey at over 40 miles an hour!

WHAT IS A SHARK'S **ENEMY?**

Nearly one-third of all shark species are threatened with **extinction.** That's mostly because of **overfishing.** But **bycatch** is a factor, too. Sharks get caught in nets set by commercial fishermen looking for other food fish, such as tuna.

Spiny dogfish

HOW MANY AND WHAT KIND OF **TEETH** DO SHARKS HAVE?

A shark can have **hundreds** of teeth. They have several rows of teeth. When a tooth breaks off, a new one moves forward to take its place. Some sharks have long, thin, **pointy** teeth used for spearing small fish. Other sharks have triangular teeth that are **serrated** like knives. These kinds of teeth cut through **flesh** and bone. Still other species have flat teeth for cracking open shellfish.

Short-fin mako shark

FRESHWATER FISH

Most people think the oceans harbor the most dangerous animals that can swim. But some fish, living in freshwater lakes and rivers, can be very scary—and deadly, too.

Those dudes need to chill out!

Despite their killer reputation, only six of the more than 60 species of piranhas are carnivorous.

Piranha

Giant catfish

WHERE DO YOU FIND
DANGEROUS
FRESHWATER FISH?

Dangerous freshwater fish are found in bodies of water on every continent except Antarctica. The **Amazon River** in South America is home to many dangerous species, including **red-bellied piranhas.** This fish is only about a foot long and weighs about 5 pounds, but it feeds in groups of up to 100. Red-bellied piranhas eat other fish but are also drawn to **disturbances** in the water. They will **aggressively attack** a struggling, sick, or injured animal, stripping the **flesh** off the animal's bones in minutes.

Red-bellied piranha

WHAT IS ONE OF THE
LARGEST FRESHWATER
FISH EVER CAUGHT?

In 2005, fishermen in northern Thailand caught a **giant catfish** in the Mekong River that was nearly **9 feet** long and weighed a monstrous **646 pounds!** It took a team of fishermen more than an hour to reel it in.

Arapaima

WHAT ARE SOME OTHER
FIERCE AMAZON
RIVER FISH?

Sometimes called the **"vampire fish,"** the payara is related to the piranha. This fish is almost 4 feet long and was named after the **6-inch-long teeth** in its lower jaw.

The **arapaima** also includes piranhas in its diet, plus birds and small animals. The arapaima is the biggest freshwater fish in the Amazon. It can grow to be up to **10 feet long** and weigh about 475 pounds. If threatened, an arapaima will leap out of the water. Some have reportedly knocked fishermen out of their boats!

SKATES AND RAYS

Skates and rays are related to sharks; they have cartilage instead of bony skeletons.

That looks like my teacher, Mr. Ray!

There are about 500 species of skate and ray. Their ancestors first swam in the world's waters about 150 million years ago.

Stingrays

WHERE ARE **SKATES** AND **RAYS** FOUND?

Skates and **rays** swim in all the oceans of the world. These fish are found both at the bottom of the sea and closer to the surface. Some rays live in freshwater. In the United States, the **Atlantic stingray** has been found in the rivers and lakes of Florida. In Thailand, the **giant freshwater stingray** has made its way into the Mekong River in the capital city of Bangkok.

Blotched fantail stingray

WHY ARE SKATES AND RAYS **SO FLAT**?

Their shape helps them to **glide** along the bottom in search of food. A skate's or ray's **mouth** is located underneath its body, so it can easily scoop up shrimp, crabs, oysters, clams, and more.

Poisonous blue-spotted stingray

HOW DOES A SKATE OR RAY **FIND ITS PREY?**

Skates and rays most likely find food using their senses of smell and hearing and the **ampullae of Lorenzini.** This is a sense organ located in the head. Sharks have it, too. It can detect the **electric fields** that animals give off.

HOW CAN YOU TELL THE **DIFFERENCE** BETWEEN A **SKATE** AND A **RAY?**

Skates and rays look very similar because both are **kite** shaped. Skates tend to have fatter tails. Only rays have **spines** on their tails. A skate typically has a large **fin** on its back. A ray has a small back fin or none at all. **Rays** tend to be larger than **skates.** Another major difference is that rays give birth to **live young.** Skates **lay eggs** in hard, rectangular sacs that are sometimes referred to as **"mermaids' purses."**

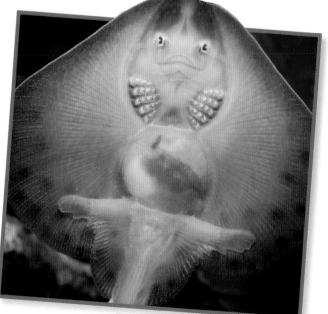

Skate hatchling

THAT'S REALLY WILD!

Blue whale

WHALES

Whales are **mammals**—not fish—that live in water. They **breathe air** through **blowholes** in their heads. There are about 83 species of whale, including dolphins and porpoises. The **orca,** also called the **killer whale,** is actually a dolphin. It got its nickname because it is known to be an aggressive **predator.** Killer whales hunt in packs and are sometimes called **"wolves of the sea."**

LARGEST
SWIMMING ANIMAL

The **blue whale** is not only the largest swimming animal, it is the world's **largest animal**—period. This aquatic mammal can be **89 feet** long and weigh over **100 tons.** A blue whale is 15 times heavier than the world's heaviest land animal, the African elephant! It eats up to **9,000** pounds of aquatic plants and animals a day—that's like eating 36,000 quarter-pound **hamburgers.**

Orca

FASCINATING ANIMALS THAT LIVE IN WATER

AND SOME WORLD-RECORD HOLDERS, TOO!

FASTEST FISH

The **sailfish** is the world's fastest fish. It swims through ocean waters at speeds up to **68** miles per hour.

Sailfish

LARGEST
TURTLE

The **leatherback sea turtle** grows to be up to 7 feet long and can weigh more than **2,000 pounds.** It is the only turtle with a leathery, flexible skin covering its top shell, or **carapace.** It can dive deeper than any other turtle, plunging to depths of **4,200** feet. A leatherback sea turtle can stay underwater for almost an hour and a half!

Leatherback sea turtle

LARGEST
AMPHIBIAN

The **Chinese giant salamander** is the world's largest **amphibian.** It can be 6 feet long and weigh **100 pounds**. It swims in rocky streams and lakes in the mountains of China.

Chinese giant salamander

VENOMOUS SEA CREATURES

There are many dangerous venomous animals living in the waters of the world. Most do not seek out people, but encounters do happen by accident.

The box jellyfish produces toxins strong enough to kill a person.

Biologist swimming with a box jellyfish

Reef stonefish

WHAT IS THE MOST
VENOMOUS FISH?

Scientists estimate there are over 1,200 species of **venomous** fish. Many consider the **stonefish** to be the most venomous of all. Looking more like a **jagged** rock than a fish, it blends into the rocky ocean floor. It lies in shallow water, waiting to **ambush** prey. The stonefish has defenses to keep it safe from larger predators, such as sharks and rays that feed off the ocean floor.

WHO IS ANOTHER
DANGEROUS FISH?

A **puffer fish,** also called a blowfish, is named for its ability to **puff up** by filling itself with water if a predator appears. Its round shape and the **spines** that pop out when it is puffed up quickly make the puffer fish unappetizing. The fish is also loaded with a powerful toxin that can be lethal. There is enough **poison** in one puffer fish to kill 30 adult humans!

Spiny puffer fish

HOW ELSE CAN A FISH BE
DANGEROUS?

The **surgeonfish** is named for the sharp, scalpel-like spine it can whip out if it feels threatened. These colorful fish, also called **tangs,** may look pretty. But they can give a sea creature—or a person—a **deep wound!**

Powder-blue tang

OCTOPUSES AND SQUID

When someone in my family hugs you, you KNOW you've been hugged!

Octopuses and squid belong to a group of animals called cephalopods. Their ancestors were around before fish swam in the oceans and mammals walked on land!

If you look at an octopus or squid, you will see that its arms are attached to its head. They don't have torsos.

Octopus

WHERE ARE THE BODY **ORGANS** OF AN **OCTOPUS OR SQUID?**

An octopus's or squid's head is actually called a **mantle**. It's a **baglike** structure that contains and protects all the body's organs, including the brain. **Cephalopods** have the largest brains of any animal without a backbone.

Big fin reef squid

WHAT IS THE PURPOSE OF **SUCKERS?**

Octopuses and squid have **eight arms.** Each arm is covered with **suckers** that help the octopus or squid hold its catch, which includes fish and crabs. An octopus or squid can also **taste** through its suckers. A **squid** has two additional tentacles that are longer than its arms.

Octopus suckers

HOW MANY **HEARTS** DOES A CEPHALOPOD HAVE?

Most cephalopods have **three hearts!** Two pump blood to the gills, and one pumps blood to the rest of the body.

WHERE DO OCTOPUSES AND SQUID **LIVE?**

They are **saltwater** creatures. They can be found in all the oceans of the world.

GLOWING
SEA CREATURES

The deeper you go in the ocean, the darker it gets. A number of fish and other creatures know how to make things a bit brighter down there—they actually produce light themselves!

It's good to keep things light, dude!

Creatures with the ability to make their own light are called bioluminescent animals.

Tube anemones

HOW DO FISH AND OTHER DEEP-SEA ANIMALS PRODUCE LIGHT?

Some fish have special organs in their bodies that are filled with **bacteria** that glow. The coral reef **flashlight fish** has these organs underneath its eyes. It can turn off the light by pushing the organ under a flap of skin.

Other fish have a special body organ called a **photophore.** The photophore is made up of cells. These use a chemical called **luciferin** to produce light. Luciferin makes light when it combines with oxygen and another chemical, called **luciferase.**

Flashlight fish

Pacific viperfish

WHAT ARE SOME BIOLUMINESCENT FISH?

The **Australian pineapple fish** has a round body covered in large, thick, yellow **protective scales.** It really does resemble a pineapple! A bacteria-filled light organ in its lower jaw makes the fish look like it's smiling.

Lantern fish produce their light with luciferin. They have **photophores** along their sides. Lantern fish use their lights to find mates and food, and to avoid predators.

Viperfish are bioluminescent fish with **photophores** along the spine and body. The jaws are filled with fanglike teeth to help hold prey once it is caught. Some scientists think the viperfish uses its light to **communicate** with other viperfish.

GLOSSARY

Ampullae of Lorenzini: a sensory organ in an elasmobranch fish's head that allows it to detect low levels of electric energy given off by other animals

Amphibian: a cold-blooded animal that spends some time in water and some time on land; most adult amphibians breathe through their skin

Animal: a living creature that can move voluntarily, find food, and digest it internally

Antibiotic: medicine taken to treat certain kinds of illnesses

Arachnid: an animal with no wings, two body parts, eight legs, and a skeleton on the outside of its body; spiders and scorpions are arachnids

Bioluminescent: having the ability to emit light

Bird: an animal with feathers and wings

Bird of prey: a flying, meat-eating animal also known as a raptor

Bycatch: an animal or animals caught unintentionally by commercial fishermen

Carapace: top shell on a turtle or tortoise

Carnivore: a meat-eating animal

Carrion: rotting flesh of a dead animal

Cartilage: tough, flexible material that makes up a shark's skeleton

Cephalopods: marine animals with large heads and tentacles; octopuses and squids are cephalopods

Cnidarians: marine animals with tentacles; jellyfish are cnidarians

Colony: a social group of animals

Constrictor: a snake that squeezes its prey to death

Crepuscular: active at dawn and dusk

Diurnal: active during daylight hours

Domesticated: accustomed to living near people

Echolocation: letting out sounds which bounce off nearby objects and back to an animal's ears

Elasmobranch: fish with cartilage; sharks, skates, and rays are elasmobranch fish

Endangered: a species of animal in danger of becoming extinct

Entomologist: someone who studies insects

Exoskeleton: a skeleton on the outside of a body; insects have exoskeletons

Extinct: when an animal species is no longer in existence

Fish: a cold-blooded animal that breathes through gills and moves through water

Guano: waste droppings; bats produce guano

Habitat: a type of place in nature, such as a forest or desert

Hibernator: an animal whose body temperature and heart rate slow and whose other body functions are suspended while the animal sleeps in a protected shelter during wintertime

Host: a living thing used by another living thing for food, to lay eggs on, or for other essential life functions; some wasps use other insects as a host for their eggs

Insect: an animal with three body parts and six legs; they may or may not have wings

Invertebrate: an animal without a backbone; a jellyfish is an invertebrate

Keratin: a fiber that makes up human hair and nails, and things such as the quills on a porcupine

Lateral line: a sensory organ all fish have to sense the vibrations of other animals moving in the water

Luciferase: a chemical that helps animals glow

Luciferin: a chemical that helps animals glow

Maggot: wormlike young of flies without legs and wings

Mammal: a warm-blooded animal covered with hair or fur; a mammal has a constant body temperature, and mammal mothers nurse their young and provide care until the young can live alone

Mantle: the head of an octopus or squid, which houses the animal's organs

Monotreme: an egg-laying mammal; there are only three monotremes—two echidna species and the duck-billed platypus

Nocturnal: active during the nighttime

Omnivore: an animal that eats both plants and meat

Ovipositor: a tubelike organ through which some animals deposit eggs; many insects have an ovipositor

Photophore: a special light-producing organ that many bioluminescent animals have

Plastron: the bottom shell of a turtle or tortoise

Predator: an animal that feeds off other animals

Prey: an animal that is hunted by other animals for food

Raptor: a bird of prey

Reptile: a cold-blooded animal covered with scaly skin; a reptile needs the sun to heat its body and give it energy

Scute: tough plates covering a turtle's or tortoise's shell

Spinneret: a tubelike structure on a spider through which it releases silk

Talons: hooked claws on a bird, such as a bird of prey

Toxin: a poison produced by a living creature

Tundra: a vast, treeless Arctic plain

Venom: a poison produced by a living creature that is injected into another creature through a bite or sting

Vertebrate: an animal with a backbone; mammals, birds, reptiles, amphibians, and fish have backbones

INDEX

PHOTO CREDITS